W9-BIR-779

For pie lovers everywhere — BB
For dearest James, with love — CS

VIKING
Published by the Penguin Group
Penguin Books USA Inc., 375 Hudson Street, New York, New York 10014, U.S.A.
Penguin Books Australia Ltd, Ringwood, Victoria, Australia
Penguin Books Canada Ltd, 10 Alcorn Avenue, Toronto, Ontario, Canada M4V 3B2
Penguin Books (N.Z.) Ltd, 182 – 190 Wairau Road, Auckland 10, New Zealand

Penguin Books Ltd, Registered Offices: Harmondsworth, Middlesex, England

First published in the United Kingdom by All Books for Children,
a division of The All Children's Company Ltd., 1993
First published in the United States of America by Viking,
a division of Penguin Books USA Inc., 1993

1 3 5 7 9 10 8 6 4 2

Text copyright © Bruce Balan, 1993
Illustrations copyright © Clare Skilbeck, 1993
All rights reserved

Library of Congress Catalog Card Number: 93-60029
ISBN 0-670-85150-7
Printed in Hong Kong

Without limiting the rights under copyright reserved above, no part of this publication may be reproduced, stored in or
introduced into a retrieval system, or transmitted, in any form or by any means (electronic, mechanical, photocopying, recording
or otherwise), without the prior written permission of both the copyright owner and the above publisher of this book.

Pie in the Sky

Written by
Bruce Balan

Illustrated by
Clare Skilbeck

Viking

It was Evelyn Plum's birthday. The Plums gave her a party.

Hilary Plum gave her mother a shovel. Gerald Plum gave his wife a left-handed doorknob. Old Seymour Plum gave his daughter a large melon. Alicia Plum gave her sister a pinecone.

Young Skip was going to give his mother a butterscotch pie, but it hadn't arrived yet.
The baker was late.
Skip stood at the window biting his lip.
Would the baker get there in time?

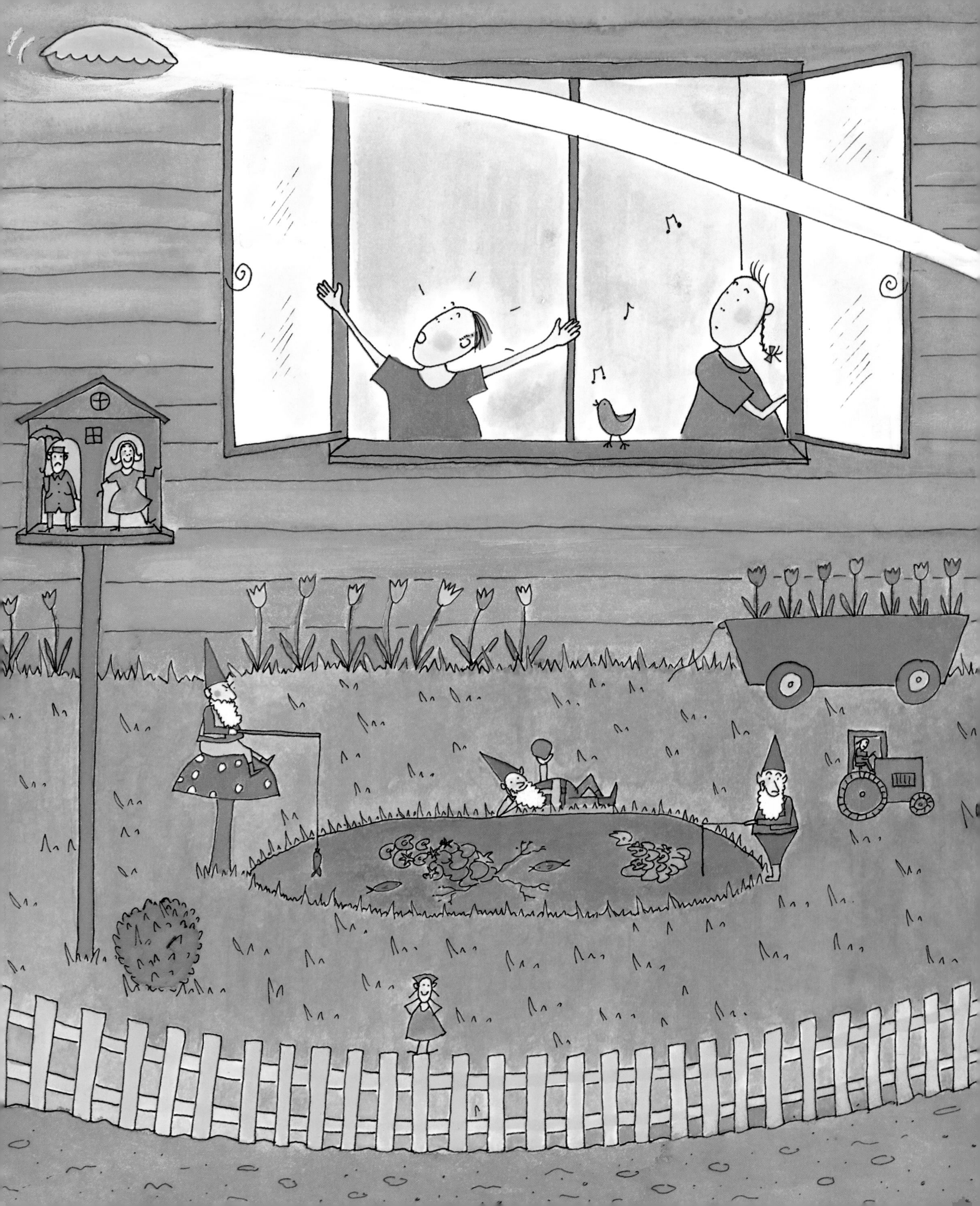

Skip heard a noise. Speeding round the corner came the baker's truck.

The baker knew he was late. Just in front of the Plums' house, he hit the brakes. But he hit them too hard. Skip's pie went flying through the air.

It did not stop.

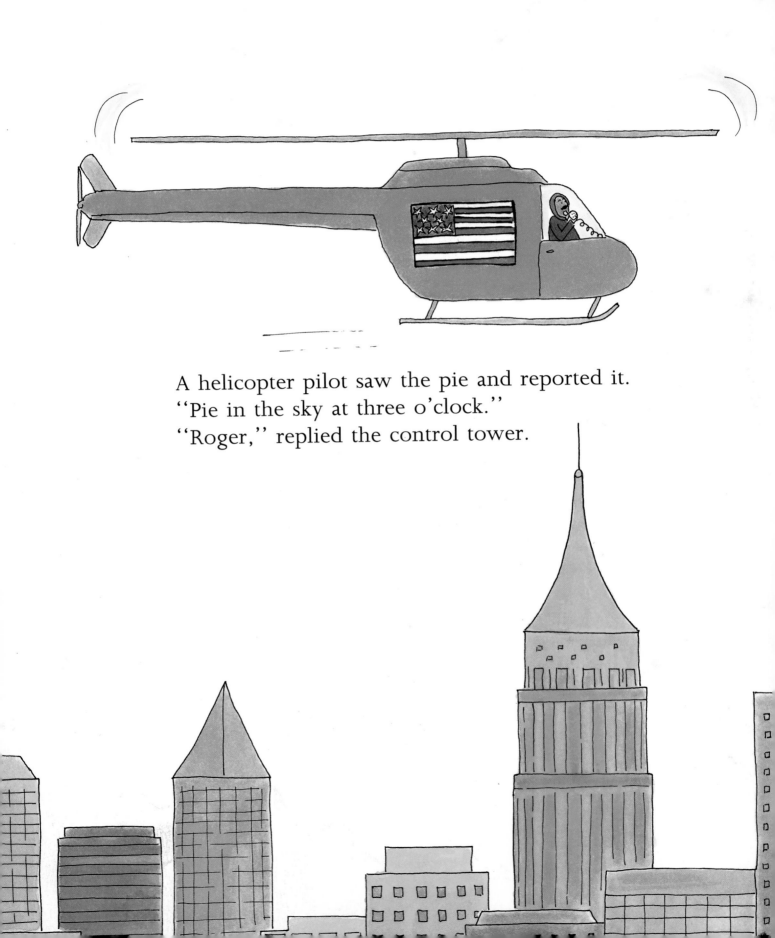

A helicopter pilot saw the pie and reported it.
"Pie in the sky at three o'clock."
"Roger," replied the control tower.

People were looking out the windows
in the Statue of Liberty's crown.
"It's a UFO!" someone shouted.

The pie sailed past the man
cleaning the dial of Big Ben.
"It must be time for tea,"
he thought.

It narrowly missed a tourist standing on the Eiffel Tower.

"There goes one of those funny French hats," she said.

In Vienna, the giant Ferris wheel was turning
around and around. People were getting dizzy.
The pie sailed past.
  Now the people were dizzy *and* confused.

At the Acropolis in Athens, tourists were taking thousands of photographs.

Tour guides were pointing at everything.

"Here are the Ionic columns! There is the Parthenon! There is the Agora! Here is the marble portico! There is a flying pie!"

It was hot in Egypt.
The pie nearly made a great splat
right in the middle of a giant face.

A fisherman off Fiji had never seen a flying pie.
"I wonder what that is?" he thought. "Looks tasty."

A cruise ship steamed across the ocean.
People were playing shuffleboard on the
deck. Some were shooting clay pigeons.
   ''There's one!''
   ''Drat! Missed it!''

Hollywood! The pie made a guest appearance in the big hit Western.

The pie flew right past Mount Rushmore.
The temptation was strong but the pie
kept going.

Evelyn Plum's party had gone on for hours.

It was getting late. It was getting cold. It was almost time for bed.

Skip sat sadly in the corner.

Mrs. Plum got up to close the window.
She looked out into the night.
   She shut her eyes and thought what a
wonderful birthday she'd had.

Splat!

Mrs. Plum smiled. Her favorite!

She hugged Skip. "Thanks," she said.
Skip smiled. "Happy Birthday, Mom."